CAMP ROCK

SECOND SESSION #3

Going Platinum

Going Platinum

By Helen Perelman

Based on "Camp Rock," Written by Karin Gist & Regina Hicks and Julie Brown & Paul Brown

Disney PRESS

New York

Printed in the United States of America

First Edition
3 5 7 9 10 8 6 4 2

Library of Congress Catalog Card Number: 2008926333
ISBN 978-1-4231-1617-2

For more Disney Press fun, visit www.disneybooks.com
Visit DisneyChannel.com

Chapter One

"Aloha! And welcome to the luau! I hope you all are ready for a fantastic night!" Brown Cesario cried. The director of Camp Rock stood on the stage in front of the lake, the summer sun setting behind him. Many of the campers were wearing grass skirts, and everyone wore a brightly colored plastic lei around his or her neck. Brown beamed as he inspected the crowd. Satisfied that everyone looked the part, he jumped off the stage. He had work to do.

"Boy, Brown is taking this pretty seriously, huh?" Mitchie Torres said to her friend Caitlyn Gellar. The two were sitting on one of the benches near the stage. "He's like a little kid at Halloween!" Mitchie eyed Brown's bright pink and yellow Hawaiian shirt as he danced over to the food table.

"Brown does love a good theme night," Caitlyn said, grinning. "Last year, he wore a Frankenstein's Monster costume for the annual Monster Mash. He painted his whole face green. It was awesome!"

Mitchie smiled. Unlike Caitlyn, who had been lucky enough to come to camp before, this was Mitchie's first summer at Camp Rock. But she already knew that Brown was wild enough to do something like dress up as a large, green monster.

Mitchie's smile grew even wider. She still couldn't believe she was here! It had been a dream come true when her mom, Connie, had gotten a job as camp cook. It got even better when Brown asked Connie to stay for the camp's second session. Mitchie would never have had such an amazing summer otherwise. She would not have met Caitlyn, Shane Gray, or all her other new friends. To Mitchie, helping out her mom in the kitchen was worth it.

"Mmm," Barron James declared as he walked over to the girls. "This is some pretty darn good cooking." He was with his best friend and music partner, Sander Loya. Together they had a soulful sound that was always a hit at any jam session. "I am so grooving on this dinner!"

Sander nodded in agreement. "And I'm *so* getting more!" he exclaimed, heading back over to the food table.

Mitchie smiled. She had helped her mom prepare the big meal. Connie took pride in selecting a menu that fit each of Brown's theme nights.

"Isn't this great?" Lola Scott asked, coming to stand between Mitchie and Caitlyn. She had a flower in her curly brown hair and a pink lei around her neck. "I love the tiki torches. It really feels tropical around here tonight." She sang a few lines from a Bob Marley song for effect.

When she stopped, Mitchie and Caitlyn stood up, and the three friends made their way over to where Brown was dancing.

"Check out Brown's moves!" Lola said. "He's a real hula superstar!"

The girls watched as he danced with Dee La Duke, their musical director. A circle had formed around the duo.

Across the circle, Mitchie caught sight of Tess Tyler. The camp diva was in a shell-shaped bikini top and a *real* grass skirt. No way would she wear a plastic one, Mitchie mused as she watched Tess sway to the beat. At Tess's side, as always, were Ella Pador and Lorraine Burgess, a new girl who had come at the start of Second Session. Lorraine had quickly become a part of Tess's entourage. She had even moved into the Vibe Cabin after Mitchie moved out to stay in the Beat Cabin with Caitlyn.

Suddenly, Peggy Dupree jumped into the circle to dance with Dee. Mitchie smiled to see her friend having so much fun. At Final Jam, Peggy had used her full name—Margaret Dupree—when she performed, and she had taken first place. Afterward, Peggy had walked away from being one of Tess's backup singers. Peggy still lived in Vibe Cabin, but she had grown closer to Mitchie and Caitlyn.

The dancing continued as Dee pulled Shane into the circle. Mitchie giggled. Shane was a guest instructor and the resident star of Camp Rock. He was also the lead singer of Connect Three, a band that was steadily climbing the pop charts. Mitchie laughed as she watched Shane try to hula. His cheeks flushed red under his thick, dark hair. But he looked relaxed—and not at all like a stuck-up rock star.

That hadn't always been true. Earlier in the year, Shane had thrown a fit about a wrong coffee order on a photo shoot. The incident had made entertainment headlines. Shane's label had sent him to Camp Rock to mellow out for the summer. Not only was Brown his uncle, but the camp was where he had gotten together with Jason and Nate, his Connect Three bandmates.

Shane had hated the idea of dropping out of the A-list scene for the summer, but the hiatus had served him well. The press on Connect Three was once again more about their music than about the spoiled behavior of their lead singer. And Shane had really been getting back to his roots, partly by working as a guest instructor and partly because he had started hanging out with Mitchie.

As Shane moved his hips the way Dee demonstrated, he caught Mitchie's eye. "C'mon, Mitchie," he called. He flashed her one of his megawatt smiles. "Let's see your moves!"

Mitchie tried not to groan. Performing in front of a crowd was still hard for her. She was better at singing or composing music alone in her cabin. Slowly, *very slowly*, she was getting more comfortable performing in front of people. But dancing the hula? That was pushing it!

Still, it was hard not to get caught up in Shane's enthusiasm. She joined him, her grass skirt swishing back and forth as she attempted to do the dance.

"Nice!" Shane called out approvingly. "You've got the beat!"

Soon, almost everyone was moving. Colby Miller grabbed Caitlyn's hand, and the two of them danced in the middle of the circle. Like Lorraine, Colby had first come to camp for

Second Session. He had quickly become friends with Mitchie and, eventually, with Caitlyn, too.

"Nice moves," Caitlyn teased him now.

Colby laughed, his eyes twinkling. "Thanks. Hey, rumor has it that Brown is making an announcement tonight. Have you heard anything?"

"You never know what Brown has up his sleeve," Caitlyn said, grinning.

"I know!" Colby agreed. "Well, whatever it is, I can't wait to hear."

Tess, who had been dancing nearby, joined in their conversation. "Maybe we're finally getting air-conditioning in the bunks," she said, fanning herself. "I requested that last summer, and I am *still* waiting."

"With all the hot air she spouts, it's no wonder she needs AC!" Caitlyn whispered in Colby's ear.

Just because her mother was T. J. Tyler, the award-winning singer, Tess thought everyone should treat *her* like a star, too. But Caitlyn had learned not to play those games with Tess a couple of summers ago.

When Mitchie first arrived at Camp Rock, Caitlyn had tried to warn her about Tess. But Mitchie hadn't listened. Instead, to impress Tess, she told everyone that her mother was a big music-television executive. Tess dropped her in a flash once the truth came out. Caitlyn almost had, too. It had taken her some time to forgive Mitchie for lying, but things were back on track.

Turning now to Tess, Caitlyn said, "I don't think that air-conditioning is the big news. But it looks like we're about to find out what is."

Brown and Dee had walked onto the stage, where a microphone was set up. Holding up his hands, Brown signaled for everyone to be silent. Caitlyn, Colby, Shane, and Mitchie moved closer so they could hear the evening's announcements.

"Is everyone having a good time?" Brown shouted. The crowd cheered loudly, and he grinned. "You know, this reminds me of the time when I was on tour in Hawaii with the Stones," Brown began.

Rolling her eyes, Caitlyn sighed. "Here we go again!" Brown loved to tell stories about when he had hung out with famous rock bands. Sometimes he went on and on, and Caitlyn was grateful when she saw Dee give Brown a gentle poke on the shoulder.

"But first, let's get through the announcements," Brown said, taking the hint from Dee. "All those in Dee's dance class, please make sure to pick up your practice CD from Keynote tonight." Brown read a few more items from his clipboard. Then he looked up and glanced around at the campers. "And now, I have a very special announcement." He extended the moment with a long pause to make sure he had everyone's attention. "This afternoon, I got some amazing news."

"It better be air-conditioning," Tess said under her breath.

"I got a call from Shane's manager," Brown went on. "And he told me that Connect Three's new album . . . just went platinum!"

The camp erupted in cheers and claps as everyone strained their necks to try and spot Shane.

For a moment, Shane just stood there, a big grin on his face. Then he picked up Mitchie and twirled her around in a circle. "I can't believe it!" he cried.

"That's incredible!" Mitchie exclaimed happily.

"Congratulations, Shane," Tess said, squirming her way in between Mitchie and Shane. "This is the big time. Really cool."

"Sorry the news isn't *cooler* for you, Tess," Caitlyn said sweetly. "Guess you'll have to keep waiting for that air-conditioning."

Tess was about to retort but thought better

of it. Turning on her flowered flip-flops, she walked off to find Ella and Lorraine.

Up on the stage, Brown was trying to get everyone quiet again. "Wait, there's more!"

The crowd hushed and waited for Brown to continue.

"In addition, the record company is so pleased with Shane's new positive press and what Camp Rock has done for him . . ." Brown went on.

"Camp Rock *rocks*!" someone cheered from the crowd.

Brown smiled. ". . . Which is why we're going to host an all-star record party for Connect Three here—at camp—this Friday night!"

The screams were deafening. Everyone began jumping around and cheering. Swept up in the excitement, Shane said good-bye to Mitchie and moved through the crowd to find his uncle.

"Can you believe this?" Caitlyn cried.

"This is going to be awesome! Think of all the stars who will come here to party with Connect Three!"

"I guess," Mitchie said uncertainly. As she watched, Shane was swarmed by everyone trying to congratulate him. Mitchie knew she should be excited and happy for Shane, but she was nervous. Sharing Shane with the world outside of camp was one thing, but having his star friends and the press come *inside* camp was a whole other story.

Chapter Two

The next morning camp was still buzzing about the big news. Rumors of who would be on the guest list were running wild, and Shane was bouncing around, happier than Mitchie had ever seen him. The old Shane would have never agreed to a party in the middle of the woods, but the new Shane seemed happy that the party was coming to *him* on his own turf.

Inside the kitchen, Mitchie and Caitlyn were working. "Would you cut up those oranges over there?" Mitchie's mom, Connie, asked the girls.

Caitlyn's kitchen duty for the summer was officially over. But she liked hanging out with Mitchie and her mom, so she helped out whenever she could. And the extra cookies she could always snag were a perk.

"Hey, ladies!" Brown called as he entered the kitchen. "How is everyone?"

Connie placed the fruit that was on her cutting board in a bowl and gave Brown a smile. "We're platinum, I hear."

"Indeed we are," Brown said with a laugh. "Have you thought about what we're going to serve all these city folks when they arrive?"

Mitchie was sure that her mom had been tossing and turning all night thinking about what she was going to serve at the party. Connie would like the event to be extra-special for Shane. Plus, she would want to make a good impression on all the visitors.

"I'm working on it," Connie said, trying to sound confident.

"Morning!" Dee sang as she waltzed into the kitchen. "I had to get my early cup of java." She headed over to the coffeemaker. "Connie, big plans for the party?"

As if her mom needed any more pressure! Mitchie watched as the line on her mother's forehead deepened.

"No worries," Connie told her, now trying to sound confident *and* calm. "We'll think of something. We always do."

Dee nodded. Turning, she looked at Brown. "Friday is the annual B's Jam. You sure you want to share the spotlight?"

"What's B's Jam?" Mitchie asked before Brown could answer.

"Only one of *the* highlights of Second Session," Caitlyn explained. "Friday is Brown's birthday, and every year we celebrate the big day with B's Jam. Four songs are picked to be performed. All original. All unplugged. No bands, no synthesizers." Caitlyn made a face. "Not my thing."

Caitlyn was all about her computer when it came to music. Her dream was to be a producer, taking a song and making it stronger with her laptop. With a few keystrokes, Caitlyn could change the sound of the music. She was really good. But she was definitely not a fan of *unplugged*—unless running her laptop on battery and Wi-Fi qualified.

"I was thinking, this year, I can pick the top four songs during Shane's songwriting session," Dee continued, still not letting Brown speak. "Those performers will go on to sing at the jam, and then the audience picks the winner."

Brown waved a hand in the air. "Of course we should still do the jam," he said. "We'll just make sure it's over before the platinum party starts."

"Great!" Dee exclaimed. "Then it's all

set!" She stood up and grabbed her mug of coffee. "And one more thing," she said. "I think that we should spruce up the place a bit today, don't you? Lots of people are coming, and the outside of the theater could use a paint job."

Brown nodded. "Good thinking, Dee. Sure. Get the troops on that this afternoon." He gave Dee a pat on the back. "Free publicity is always good for business!"

After Brown and Dee walked out, Mitchie turned to Caitlyn. "Do you think I have a chance of winning B's Jam? I haven't won a jam yet this summer!"

"It's practically made for you," Caitlyn said. "But they have to be all new songs, so you better get writing."

"I'm sure Shane's songwriting session tomorrow is going to be packed, huh?" Mitchie asked. Anyone who wanted to sing in the jam would probably be there.

Nodding her head, Caitlyn agreed. "You

have to stay focused and not worry about everyone else. I bet you have a few surprises locked up in your song journal."

Mitchie nodded. Her journal was not just filled with daily events and drawings like some other people's. It was mostly filled with lyrics, music notes, and uncompleted phrases. Hopefully the contents would inspire her to write one of her best songs yet.

"I really want to do this," Mitchie said to Caitlyn and her mom.

"Then you will," Connie replied, giving her daughter a hug. "And I'm not just saying that because I'm your mom." She grinned at her own catchphrase. "Now go eat your fruit and pancakes with the rest of the rock stars."

After breakfast was over, Dee roped in most of the campers to help out with painting the theater. Out of the corner of her eye, Mitchie saw Shane check out the scene. He quickly ducked behind a bush, hoping to sneak by.

But Dee saw him, too. Caught, Shane walked up and Mitchie handed him a brush and a bucket of paint.

"Thanks," he said. He dipped the brush in the bucket, swishing the paint around. "I think this party is going to be really cool. Definitely different than the typical record-label parties."

"That's for sure," Mitchie said, dipping her own brush into the paint.

"I heard that all the top producers and stars are coming," Tess said, approaching Shane and Mitchie. Ella and Lorraine trailed behind her. Tess held a small bucket of paint with one finger, a look of disgust on her face. She couldn't believe she was painting! At home, there were people to do that for her. Sighing, she went on. "My mom would totally be here, Shane, but she's in Europe right now."

Mitchie knew what was coming. Tess was about to go on and on about all her best friends in the business who would be coming to see Shane . . . and her, of course. Tess didn't disappoint.

"My mother said that Lily Rain is planning to attend," Tess boasted, talking about another big star. "And if Lily comes, then I am sure Zack Beslow will come, too." Tess fanned herself with her hand. "He was at one of my birthday parties, you know."

"I actually don't think those guys are coming," Shane said, unaffected by Tess's report. "Lily and Zack would break out in hives if they had to be out of the city lights for more than an hour." He laughed. "But my manager is stoked with the responses he has gotten. He says that it's gonna be a huge party."

"How many people?" Ella asked. Today, she had matched her lip gloss to her neon pink tank top.

"More than this camp has seen in a long time," Shane replied.

"Then all the more reason to make sure we

get this building painted," Dee said, walking up behind them. "I want this camp to look its best."

Mitchie let out a big sigh. More than the camp had seen in a long time? It made her stomach flip-flop. Unlike everyone else at camp, this platinum party was beginning to make her feel more dull than shiny.

Chapter Three

Later that evening, Caitlyn found Mitchie sitting on the porch of their cabin, journal in hand. Caitlyn shook her head. She should have known that Mitchie would have her nose in that book. "Hey, how's it going?" she asked as she approached. "You disappeared after dinner. Shane was asking where you went, and I've been looking all over for you!"

"I wanted to try to write something,"

Mitchie admitted. "But I can't seem to find the right words—or even a tune."

"I bet a late-night snack would help you out," Caitlyn said. She put out her hand and pulled her friend up. "I happen to know where there might be some cookies to give you the inspiration you need."

Clutching her journal in one hand, Mitchie followed Caitlyn to the mess hall. When they walked inside, they found Connie sitting at one of the islands. She was hunched over a notepad, crumpled papers surrounding her.

"Don't tell me you're trying to write a song, too!" Caitlyn exclaimed.

Connie looked up, her expression exhausted. "Hardly!" she said. "I'm trying to figure out a menu suitable for a platinum celebration. Do you realize how few platinum-colored foods there are?"

Mitchie and Caitlyn shrugged. "Hmm, I never really thought about it before," Mitchie observed as she slid into a chair next to her mother.

"Looks like you need a bit of chocolate-chip inspiration," Caitlyn sang out. She marched over to the pantry and grabbed a container of freshly made cookies. "A little chocolate goes a long way." She extended the box to Connie and then to Mitchie.

"Maybe you're right," Connie said, taking a big bite of the cookie. She got up and began to pace. "I'll take inspiration anywhere I can get it right now. I have to present the final menu to Brown first thing tomorrow morning to get my food order in on time." Looking over, she noticed Mitchie's glum expression. "How's the writing coming, sweetie?" she asked.

"I've got nothing," Mitchie said with a sigh as she took a handful of cookies.

Swinging herself up on the counter, Caitlyn looked over at Connie's pad. "Neither does your mom. You don't have *any* ideas you like?" she asked, noting the lines of crossed out words.

"Could be too limiting to do only platinum foods," Mitchie commented. "Maybe you should branch out."

"What about using a million copies sold as a theme?" Caitlyn suggested. "That's what going platinum means."

Connie's eyes widened. "That's a great idea!" She raced back over to her pad, pencil in hand. Then she stopped. "A million what, though?"

They all laughed and passed the cookies around one more time.

"I have to wonder, even if it is a great hook, why would any of these A-list record people want to come to a camp in the middle of the woods?" Connie mumbled. "They have elaborate, expensive parties all the time. They're used to red carpets, not dirt paths."

"Hey, what's wrong with camp?" Caitlyn said defensively. "You are talking about MY camp here. The lake, the spirit, the music, the cookouts!"

Mitchie jumped up. "That's it!" she cried. "That's the perfect theme!"

Connie and Caitlyn stared at Mitchie in confusion. They had no clue what she was talking about.

"Don't you see?" Mitchie asked. "*Camp* is the theme! All the great foods at camp—s'mores, hot dogs, hamburgers, bug juice . . ."

"Chocolate-chip cookies," Caitlyn added. "I get it. Go rustic. Go camp. Go real."

The girls waited to see Connie's reaction. She looked up at the ceiling as she considered the idea. Then a smile spread across her face. "That's brilliant," she said, walking over to embrace her daughter. She reached out and pulled Caitlyn into the hug, too. "Oh, you girls are the best."

"What's the best?" Brown said as he opened the door, clipboard in hand. He had been craving a treat and saw the light on.

"The theme for the party Friday night," Caitlyn said, grinning.

As Connie described the menu, Brown grabbed a cookie and nibbled on the treat. "That all sounds delicious. I love it!" He slid his clipboard onto the counter and applauded. "A standing ovation! Is that why you called this meeting?"

Connie bowed and then blushed. "Sort of," she said. "These girls have been a great help."

"So what are you looking at?" Caitlyn asked, moving a little closer to Brown. He had placed his clipboard on the counter. "The RSVPs for the party!" she exclaimed when she saw what was attached to the board. She *had* to find out who was coming!

"We should have quite a crowd here," Brown said, nodding. "Camp Rock has always had starry nights, but this party is going to bring out a new kind of stargazing! It is going to be amazing."

"Well, before everyone gets here," Connie said, "I'd like you to take a look at that ice-maker in the back room. It hasn't been working so well, and if it's warm Friday night everyone is going to want cold drinks."

Brown walked over to the back room. "No worries. I'll take a look now," he said. "Show me the problem."

As soon as Brown and Connie were out of the kitchen, Caitlyn whipped around to face Mitchie. "Okay, quick," she said. "You watch the door while I check out the list." She lunged forward to grab Brown's clipboard.

"Caitlyn! What are you doing?" Mitchie squeaked. "If Brown catches you . . ."

"Which is why you need to watch the door in case he comes back in here," Caitlyn said. She looked beseechingly at Mitchie. "C'mon, don't you want to know who's coming?" How could Mitchie not care? Caitlyn was dying to know!

Mitchie shrugged. For her, B's Jam was the

main event on Friday. It was her chance to finally prove that she had what it took to win a jam.

Of course, she wanted to be at the party for Shane and support him. But impressing the A-listers was not her thing. People like Tess were into that—as was the old Shane. But not the new Shane, and definitely not Mitchie. She had learned her lesson about pretending to be someone she wasn't during the first session!

Caitlyn's eyes scanned the list. "Oh, my," she said. "This is incredible." She flipped through more pages and then her finger paused on a name. "Faye Hart?" Caitlyn's eyes widened. She looked over at Mitchie. "Faye Hart is coming here?"

Mitchie stared at Caitlyn. "Faye Hart who has that annoying single, 'Bubbling Sunshine'?"

"The one and only," Caitlyn said, sliding the clipboard back to where Brown had left it. "Also known as Shane's old girlfriend."

"Shane dated Faye Hart?" Mitchie asked. Suddenly, she *did* care about the RSVP list—very much.

Caitlyn walked over to her. Was it possible that Mitchie didn't know that Shane and Faye had been an "it" couple? And, that last she had heard, they were still friends? "You really don't read magazines, do you?" Caitlyn put her hand on Mitchie's arm. "They were only about the hottest couple for most of last year. The magazines were always showing them together. And their breakup was well documented in the tabloids."

Mitchie exhaled. "Well, they broke up. So it's totally not a big deal."

"Not according to the *Music Beat* magazine that Ella had last week," Caitlyn reported. "They had an interview with Faye saying how she missed Shane terribly and that she would be coming up to visit him at camp. I can't believe that story was true! I bet Ella my once-a-week gummi-worm fix from the canteen that the story was false. Man!" Caitlyn groaned in disappointment. She loved going to B-Note and stocking up on the chewy snacks.

Mitchie's heart started to race. But then she calmed herself. She and Shane had something special, and she wasn't going to ruin it by freaking out over nothing. "Shane hasn't said a word about this. Which means that even if she is coming, he doesn't care."

"Maybe," Caitlyn said. But her tone implied that she didn't believe that at all.

"Or maybe Shane doesn't even know!" Mitchie exclaimed. "It's not like he's paying close attention to any of the details of the party. I bet he doesn't even know that she RSVP'd."

Caitlyn nodded. "That's definitely possible." She tried to sound upbeat for her friend's sake, but she wasn't sold on that theory for one second.

Putting her cookie down, Mitchie frowned. She wasn't sold either. It was going to take much more than chocolate to solve this problem. She had to talk to Shane. He would put her mind at ease—she hoped.

Chapter Four

The stage by the lake was filling up quickly with anxious songwriters. More people than usual were piling onto the benches in front for the start of Shane's morning writing class.

Mitchie had stayed up late the night before working on her song. Call it inspiration or call it a competitive nature, but the idea that Faye was coming to Camp Rock had jump-started her creative juices. After her cookie binge, she had taken a walk along the path by the lake. The words and melody had come easily, and she had quickly jotted them down in her song journal. She had been thinking about the cocoon that camp had become for her and how she felt being with Shane, surrounded by trees and birds and no pressure. The result was, "This Place." And she was really, really happy with the song.

Now she sat with her legs tucked under her, reviewing her chord choices as the rest of the campers settled in, waiting for Shane to arrive. Beside her, Caitlyn fiddled with her laptop.

In the row behind them, Tess, Lorraine, and Ella were occupying themselves while they waited. "Did you read this?" Lorraine asked Ella. The girl's freckled nose was buried deep in the newest issue of *Music Beat*.

Ella looked over her shoulder to see what

article Lorraine was talking about. Ella's parents sent her a copy of the magazine every week, and she read the issue cover to cover before passing it on to her cabinmates.

"Isn't it amazing?" Ella said, when she saw which piece it was. "I mean, I kind of feel like we're mentioned in the article. How cool are we?" She flipped open a mirror and applied some fresh frosted lip gloss.

Tess looked up from filing her nails. "What are you talking about?"

Ella took the magazine from Lorraine's hands. "'Faye Hart has been missing Shane Gray around town,'" she read. "'Rumor has it that Faye is planning a visit to Camp Rock to see one of the camp's brightest stars at the record label's rocking platinum celebration this week.'"

Rolling her eyes, Tess sighed. "And how does that translate to include you?"

Ella blushed. "Well, I am a star at Camp Rock."

"A star in your own mind, maybe," Caitlyn mumbled from her spot beside Mitchie.

"Well, of course Faye is coming to the party," Tess replied with an air of authority. "She's one of the hottest pop singers on the charts. She's not going to miss *the* party of the summer—or the chance to get back together with Shane." Tess slipped her nail file in her pocket and looked at her friends. "Faye is such a sweetheart. You'll all love her."

"You know Faye Hart?" Lorraine asked, mesmerized.

"Oh, yeah," Tess said. "She's really cool. I just know that she's going to love my new song. When I win B's Jam, she'll get a chance to see some true talent—maybe we'll even do a duet together."

"And what makes you so sure you're winning B's Jam?" Barron asked playfully, joining the girls on the bench. "Besides, the jam will be over before Shane's party gets under way. No one is coming to hear *your* music. They're coming to celebrate Shane and Connect Three."

"Whatever," Tess said. Shrugging, she turned around to aim her face up at the sun. "All I know is you can bet that Faye is coming to see Shane, not for the publicity like some of these other stars," she said matter-of-factly. "She wants to get Shane back."

Mitchie felt numb. Why hadn't Shane told her about Faye? Before her mind could spin out of control, she tried to remember the last time she had seen Shane alone. It had been a while, and he *had* been preoccupied. Maybe he just hadn't had the chance to tell her.

"Hello there, songbirds," Shane called out, startling Mitchie. He walked toward the stage with a water bottle in hand and sunglasses shading his dark eyes. "I see we have a few extra people here this morning." He grinned at the campers. "I guess everyone wants to make a good impression at B's Jam, so let's not waste any time," he said. He took a swig of his water and sat down in the front row. "Who wants to go first?"

Barron's hand shot up. "We have something we'd like to share," he said, motioning to Sander.

"Cool," Shane replied. He adjusted his sunglasses and nodded for the two boys to begin.

As Mitchie listened to the song, she felt a wave of doubt wash over her. Barron and Sander were so confident. Even without any instruments, their song sounded amazing. She looked down at her guitar beside her. Would she sound that good?

When they were done, Shane offered some suggestions that seemed to make the boys pretty happy. They traded high fives and went off under a tree to rework the second verse.

"Mitchie," Shane said. "What do you have hiding in your journal?"

Mitchie blushed. She looked over at Caitlyn,

who gave her an encouraging smile. "It's called 'This Place,'" she said softly.

Taking another sip of water, Shane nodded his head. "I like the title. So let's see if I like the sound."

Mitchie reached beside her and picked up her guitar. When she was settled on the stage, she began strumming softly. As she got into the melody of the song, the people around her faded from her vision, and she thought only about Shane and camp.

"And it's here where I can breathe.
Where I can be me, and I am free.
This place, it's not mine or yours forever.
But let's stay and live on borrowed time
for a while."

When Mitchie sang the last note there was absolute silence. No one said a word. Shane took off his sunglasses and looked right into Mitchie's eyes.

"That was beautiful," he said. "Did you just write that?"

Feeling her face grow warm, Mitchie looked down. "Last night," she said.

Caitlyn let out a loud cheer. Mitchie had rocked her song!

Mitchie sighed with relief. Writing a song was like putting together a jigsaw puzzle. When the pieces fit and the picture was complete, it was worth all the effort.

Lola went next and sang her heart out, as she always did.

"Wow," Peggy said to Mitchie when she returned to her seat. Peggy had been quictly sitting, waiting her turn. But after Mitchie's song—and now Lola's—she was feeling a little nervous. "Lola's song was amazing."

"She's really good," Mitchie said, agreeing. "But, wait! You can't be worried! You won Final Jam—you're a total star!"

Peggy didn't say anything. Ever since she had stood up to Tess at Final Jam last session, she'd felt a lot of pressure. Yes, she'd won the jam, but each competition was different. And she had grown used to singing backup for Tess. It was unnerving to be on her own—which is why she still sang with Tess, Ella, and Lorraine on occasion.

"Hey, Peggy," Shane called. "You're up. Ready?"

Shane focused on Peggy, and she took her music sheet in her hands. She had just finished writing the song that morning. But when she started to sing, her whole heart was in it. When she finished, everyone applauded. Except for Tess. Peggy smiled, relieved. She actually took that as a compliment.

When the songwriting class came to an end, everyone went on to their next activity. Mitchie hung back to walk with Shane. They fell into step, and for a moment they were quiet, just enjoying being together.

"I really liked that song," Shane said, breaking the silence. He raised his eyebrows inquisitively. "Your inspiration?"

"Oh, just somc place I know," she answered coyly.

Shane gave her a playful push and smiled. "Well, good work," he said. "B's Jam is totally up your alley. You sound great with the guitar."

"Thanks," Mitchie said softly. They walked on. She wanted to ask Shane a million questions about Faye, but she bit her tongue. If Shane wanted to tell her something he would, right?

Once again, it was Shane who broke the silence. "This party Friday night is going to be out of hand," he said as they walked down the path to the lake. "I can't believe how many people are coming."

"Yeah, it sounds great," Mitchie managed to say. She kicked a pebble on the ground with her toe.

"I just saw the guest list this morning," Shane went on.

Mitchie stopped walking. Shane had only seen the list that morning! So he *hadn't* known!

"Faye is coming," he said, as if reading Mitchie's mind. "I'd love to see her try to walk on this path with her fancy, high-heeled shoes. You can take the girl out of the city, but you can't take the city out of the girl!" He laughed again but stopped when he realized that Mitchie wasn't laughing along with him. "Oh, right, you don't know Faye Hart, do you?"

"Oh, not unless you count reading about her in the pages of *Music Beat*," Mitchie said. "And about how much she misses you."

Shane turned to face Mitchie, his brown eyes serious. "Believe me," he said, "Faye and I are long over. We haven't spoken in months." He looked at Mitchie's face. "I'm sure she is just coming for the potential headlines. You aren't upset, are you?"

"Not now," Mitchie answered, smiling

broadly. Suddenly she felt like she could breathe again. Shane and Faye were history. And she and Shane were solid. She almost giggled with relief. Instead, she changed the subject. “But I *am* nervous about the tryouts for Brown’s birthday. I haven’t won a jam yet. I’d really love to be one of the performers Friday night.”

A smile spread across Shane’s handsome face. “With your song, you have an excellent chance,” he said. “I’ve got to run up to the office. I’ll catch you later, okay?”

“You bet,” Mitchie said, waving good-bye. She swung her guitar over her shoulder and rushed to her dance class, humming her song the whole way. Things were looking up.

Chapter Five

The next morning, the vibe on the stage by the lake was a little different than it had been the previous day. Instead of reading magazines, gossiping, and suntanning, most of the campers had gathered to rehearse their songs before Dee arrived.

Peggy tapped her foot and tried to stay calm. She hoped that Dee would hurry up. She didn't want to lose her nerve!

Mitchie was just as nervous. She was pacing up and down the sandy lakefront area.

"Hey, Mitchie, are you ready?" Caitlyn called, running up to her friend.

"I don't know," Mitchie answered. "There's so much pressure!"

Caitlyn grabbed her hand. "You are going to be fine. More than fine. Your song is amazing. You had everyone talking yesterday." She smiled encouragingly. "You're really good, Mitchie. This jam is yours. First, you just need to get past Dee."

Hugging her guitar, Mitchie looked at Caitlyn. "Thanks," she said. "I appreciate the support."

"Hey, Dee is here!" Lola shouted. She waved her arms to get Mitchie and Caitlyn's attention. "Come on, let's get this party started!"

Dee was walking up the path with Shane. They were talking and laughing as if nothing special was about to happen. Mitchie took a deep breath as the two took their seats. This was a moment she'd been waiting for . . . it was her chance to shine with all the stars at Camp Rock.

"All right, folks," Dee called. "I have the list here from Shane, so let's start. I'll listen to all the songs and let you know the results at dinner tonight. The top four singers will head to the theater for rehearsal directly after dishes are cleaned."

"We are so there!" Sander said as he traded a high five with Barron.

Peggy twisted a strand of her long black hair around her finger. She wished that she felt as confident as Barron and Sander. She sat a little taller in her seat and tried to concentrate on her breathing. I am Margaret Dupree, she said to herself. I can do this! When it was finally her turn, she began to sing. At the end of the song, Dee wrote comments without looking up from her clipboard. Peggy walked back to her seat and let out a deep sigh. She had done it. Now she would just have to wait and see.

"Mitchie Torres, you're next," Dee said.

Mitchie took her spot onstage. She put her hand on the neck of the guitar and began to pluck out the first notes. Glancing up, she caught Shane's eye. He winked at her, and suddenly she felt a surge of confidence. This was her place, her time. She began to sing.

When she was finished, Dee wrote more notes. What did Dee think? Mitchie wondered as she put her guitar back in the case. Fingers crossed, she slid next to Caitlyn to listen to the others perform.

Mitchie stared at the afternoon light sparkling off the lake. In a few hours, she'd know if she was going to be one of the final four to perform. She pulled her brown hair up into a ponytail. It was going to be a long day.

* * *

The mess hall was extraloud that night. It was the eve of Shane's big party and B's Jam—no one could be quiet.

Finally, after everyone had eaten, Dee got up and took the microphone. "As I'm sure you know, I've got an announcement," she shouted to the crowd. In record time, the room grew quiet. Dee smiled. "That's more like it," she remarked. She held up her clip-board and without further ado, read the names of the finalists.

"Peggy, Sander and Barron, Lola, and Mitchie," she said. "You have all been chosen for the annual B's Jam tomorrow night. As I told you earlier, rehearsals are in the theater directly after dinner."

As soon as Dee was done, Mitchie leaped out of her seat. Turning, she hugged her friends and then caught Shane's eye. He gave her a thumbs-up. Mitchie smiled.

"We're in!" Lola squealed. She grabbed

Mitchie's and Peggy's arms. "Can you believe we are all in this together? Wild!"

Peggy was in shock! She had not moved since her name was called. Finally, the words sunk in, and she let out a squeal. Making it to the finals in B's Jam was almost as great as winning Final Jam. "We're in! We're in!" she chanted.

From her seat, Tess grumbled. "Whatever," she said, shrugging. "Who wants to be in an acoustic jam anyway?"

"I thought you did," Ella said, skillfully applying her lip gloss without the aid of a mirror.

Tess shot her an evil look and stormed out of the mess hall.

Peggy had to smile at Tess's dramatic exit. Her song had been typical—over the top and showy. For B's Jam, it didn't fit. Of course, Tess didn't see things that way. She was *always* supposed to win.

After all the dishes were cleared away,

Peggy, Lola, Sander, Barron, and Mitchie ran over to the theater. It was great to be back in the space where Final Jam had taken place. Mitchie felt like she was floating.

Dee was waiting for the performers at center stage.

"Congratulations," Dee said. "You all wrote amazing songs. I believe that this is going to be one of the best jams we've had. I'm really excited."

"Me, too!" Peggy shouted.

"So let's pick numbers out of this hat to see the order." Dee held out a Camp Rock baseball cap and passed it around. "We'll run through each of your songs tonight so you get a feel for the place and its acoustics without any other instruments or synthesizers."

After they each picked a number, the order was decided. Peggy would go first, then Barron and Sander, Lola next, and Mitchie last. Peggy and Lola were both playing piano, and Sander and Barron weren't using any instruments. Mitchie was the only one with a guitar.

They ran through the first two songs. Since everyone else was still at the evening activity, the theater was quiet. There were only rows of empty benches. But as Mitchie got up, Shane walked in and sat down on one of the side benches. Mitchie was relieved to see him. His presence gave her confidence.

She had just opened her mouth to sing when there was a commotion at the door. A few people were walking in from outside. Dee went over to ask them to keep quiet.

"Go ahead, Mitchie," Shane called out.

Mitchie nodded and started singing.

"And it's here where I can breathe.
Where I can be me, and I am free.
This place, it's not mine or yours forever.
But let's stay and live on borrowed time
for a while."

She kept singing, hoping that her concentration wouldn't be broken by the commotion. But it was impossible. She lost her place and forgot the words to one of the verses.

"Keep going, Mitchie," Dee encouraged. "I'm sorry for this rude interruption." She glared at the girl and the three men beside her who had disrupted things.

By then, Shane had stood up. "Faye?" he asked, squinting. "Faye, what are you doing here?"

Mitchie's heart slammed against her chest. Faye Hart was here? Already?!

"I was trying to surprise you!" the pop star shouted. She flicked her long, stick-straight blond hair away from her face. "Who knew that this theater was harder to get into than Cool Jay's party on the Strip?" She barreled past Dee and went over to embrace Shane. Her strappy, gold high-heeled shoes clicked on the wooden floor.

Laughing at the girl's exuberance, Shane gave Faye a big hug hello. But a look from Dee prevented them from speaking. Without another word, they went and sat down. The three men remained at the back of the theater.

"I'm so sorry, Mitchie," Dee said. "Please start at the beginning." Then she turned to Shane. "And please, no more interruptions."

Now Mitchie was feeling not only very nervous but very annoyed. Why was Faye already at camp? The party wasn't until tomorrow night. And why was she practically sitting in Shane's lap, drooling all over him?

When the song was over, Faye leaped to her feet. "That song had such a great vibe to it," she cooed. "Dean, wasn't that good?" She turned to one of the three guys now huddled by the door. The tallest one must have been Dean, because he stepped forward.

"Very cool," he said. "Good lyrics, and I like the melody."

The other two men nodded.

Faye walked over to Mitchie. "I really loved it. And I want to have it. How much would it cost?" She stood at the edge of the stage grinning sweetly up at Mitchie. Mitchie was pretty sure Faye was somebody who usually got what she wanted.

Hugging her guitar close to her, Mitchie stared at Faye. "Well, I'm not sure it's for sale," she finally replied.

"What?" Faye squealed. "Oh, come on." She narrowed her eyes. "Do you know who you're talking to? Do you know what it would mean if *I* sang *your* song?"

"I've got a pretty good idea," Mitchie mumbled. She jumped off the stage and went over to put her guitar in the case.

"Hey, Faye," Shane said, stepping in. "Come on, leave her alone."

Annoyed, Faye spun around. Her blue eyes had gone from warm to icy. "I'm serious, Shane. I'm scheduled to perform at your party tomorrow night. I'd love to sing this song. Wouldn't that be so perfect for *me* to sing that to *you* here?"

Mitchie wanted to shout, No! That would be all wrong! Faye's sound was full of synthesizers and pulsing dance beats. "This Place" was not her type of song at all.

"Seriously, I really, *really* want to have it," Faye said to Mitchie, switching back to an overly sweet tone. "I think this could make a great single on my new album."

The three guys at the door pulled out cell phones as though they could instantly make this request happen.

"Well, you have until tomorrow morning," Faye barked when Mitchie didn't say anything. "I'll have Dean write up the papers." Faye tossed her shiny hair from side to side. Then she focused her blue eyes on Shane. "Come on, sweetie, I have some presents for you in my car." She reached out and grabbed his arm. Before Mitchie could even utter a word, Faye had pulled Shane out of the theater and into the dark night.

"Whoa," Barron said, when she was gone. "That was intense."

"I can't believe Faye Hart wants to sing *your* song, Mitchie!" Peggy exclaimed. "Aren't you totally psyched?"

"I don't know," Lola said before Mitchie could answer. "That girl looks like trouble to me. And Mitchie's song is not her style at all. Personally, I think that she just wants Shane to look at her the way he was looking at Mitchie when she was singing it!"

Mitchie's jaw dropped. "What?" she asked, wrenching her gaze from the door Shane had disappeared through. Could Lola be right? Was Faye jealous of *her*? How could that possibly be?

"Yeah," Sander said, nodding his head thoughtfully. "I could believe that. But if that girl is going to write a check for the song, I say take it to the bank!"

Mitchie closed her guitar case and grasped the handle. "It's not for sale."

She walked out of the theater and into the dark night with one thought on her mind: what would be the cost of saying no to Faye Hart?

Chapter Six

When Mitchie got to breakfast the next morning, Shane wasn't sitting at his usual table. She sat stirring her cereal around and around in her bowl, watching the door. Completely absorbed in her own world, she barely noticed when Caitlyn slipped onto the bench next to her.

"Jason and Nate came in early this morning," Caitlyn told her. She reached over and grabbed a banana from the fruit bowl in front of Mitchie. "Now that Connect Three is here, it's all about the press and the party. Shane's sitting on a temporary 'stage' in the center of camp. He's giving interviews—in case you were wondering."

"Oh," Mitchie said, sighing. That explained his absence.

Caitlyn gave Mitchie's shoulder a squeeze. She knew her friend was feeling confused. Before lights-out last night, Mitchie had filled her in on the crazy rehearsal and on Faye's surprise appearance—and offer. "For what it's worth," Caitlyn told her now, "I think that you should hear what Faye has to say. You don't even know what she is offering. It's just business."

"I really don't want her to sing that song," Mitchie mumbled. How could she explain? The song was personal. "And my music isn't 'just business.'"

"But it could mean a lot of publicity,"

Peggy said, joining their conversation. She slid down the bench closer to Mitchie. "Publicity that people like us can usually only dream about. Caitlyn's right. You have to at least listen to what Faye has to say."

Mitchie knew that her friends had a point. This could be the chance of a lifetime. She pushed her bowl away. "All right," she said. "I'll hear what she has to say."

"Great!" Caitlyn exclaimed. "Do you want me to go with you? I could be like your agent."

Mitchie smiled. "I'd rather you come along as my friend," she said.

"You got it!" Caitlyn replied. "We'll meet after first activity, okay?"

Mitchie and Caitlyn finished breakfast and said good-bye to Peggy. Walking out of the dining hall, the girls ran right into a mob of reporters. Even though the party wasn't until that evening, the press was getting a head start. Word of Faye's early arrival had already leaked, and the whole vibe of the camp had changed. It was suddenly more red-carpet affair than down-home country living.

Tess was standing under a tree, eagerly answering an interviewer's questions. Where most of the campers seemed annoyed by the disruption, Tess soaked up the flash of camera bulbs like sunlight.

"Yes, it's been great catching up with Faye," Tess said to one reporter as Mitchie and Caitlyn walked by. "We've been friends for years."

Giggling, Caitlyn whispered to Mitchie, "Yeah, that's why Faye hasn't said a word to her since she arrived!"

But Mitchie wasn't paying attention to Tess and her phantom celebrity status; her eyes were focused on the center of camp, where she saw Connect Three being questioned by several reporters. When Shane saw Mitchie, he waved. But when he tried to get up, his manager gave him a stern look and he stayed in his seat.

"I'll meet you right here at the end of the class, okay?" Caitlyn said when they arrived outside Keynote, one of the camp's rehearsal cabins. Mitchie had a guitar class while Caitlyn was heading off for an independent activity.

"Thanks," Mitchie said. She was glad to have Caitlyn by her side. She had thought about going to talk to her mom, but Connie was so busy with the party preparations Mitchie hadn't wanted to bother her. She would have to fill her in later. If Faye *did* want to buy the song, there was no way Mitchie would sell without her mom's okay. Sighing, she entered the cabin. Maybe practice would take her mind off things—at least for a little while.

As promised, Caitlyn was standing right outside Keynote when Mitchie came out.

"Come on," Caitlyn said, taking Mitchie's hand. "Let's go the back way. I can't believe how many reporters are here. This place is crawling with them!"

The girls went through the woods, quickly making their way to the cabin where Faye was rehearsing for her performance.

"How do you know where to go?" Mitchie asked, amazed that Caitlyn could find her way through the thick bushes and trees with no apparent path.

"One summer, I had a crush on this guy," she said, giggling. "I used to spy on him! And this was the best, and fastest, route!"

Sure enough, a bunk came into view on the left, right next to the rehearsal cabin where Faye was singing. Mitchie smiled.

"Nice work," she said.

When they walked inside, the girls heard Faye whining to Dean. "What is it with this place? Haven't they heard of air-conditioning?"

Mitchie laughed to herself. Maybe Faye and Tess *were* friends.

"Oh, great!" Faye shouted when she saw the two girls at the door. "You came! Dean, take the sheet music and see what we've got here. Joe, will you do a key check? And Steve, can you get Phil on the phone?"

The shortest of the three men in black and dark glasses was apparently Steve. He walked over to Mitchie. "Hi," he said. "Could you go ahead and sing the song again for us. I have to plug in Faye's manager in New York. He wants to hear you sing it first."

"Oh, um . . . Well, I . . ." Mitchie started to stutter. She was here to listen to an offer, not audition the song!

"Sure, she'll be ready in a minute," Caitlyn said, giving Mitchie a push toward the stage. "You can do this," she assured her as Steve began dialing the number. "Consider it practice for tonight's jam."

A moment later, Steve walked over to

Mitchie. "Listen, can you hang out for a little bit? We've got to wait for Phil to get off a call. Shouldn't be too long."

Mitchie checked her watch. She had to be in the kitchen in about twenty minutes. Not only did her mom have to serve lunch to the camp today, but she was swamped with making hamburgers and other treats for the growing number of party guests. Mitchie had promised that she'd help out. She hoped this Phil guy would call back soon.

As Faye paced the room, her shoes clicking and clacking, her entourage followed her. *She seems to have everyone wrapped around her finger,* Mitchie mused. *Does that include Shane?* Shaking her head, Mitchie pushed the thought aside.

The sound of Faye's latest song filled the room as Steve's cell phone rang and he motioned that it was time for Mitchie to start. Closing her eyes, she began. She sang it as if she were singing to Shane and they were together by the lake. When she was finished, there was silence. She looked over at Caitlyn who smiled and gave her a thumbs-up.

Faye took the phone from Steve's hand and turned her back to them. Mitchie tried to hear what she was saying, but Faye was speaking quietly, her hands gesturing wildly. Finally, she spun around. "Okay, Phil is totally on board. We just need the music and we'll get started. Steve, get Simon on the phone, and Dean, see if you can change the key. And could someone please get me a bottle of water!"

"Wait, I didn't agree to anything yet," Mitchie said. She took her sheet music off the stand and stood back.

"Listen, I can make you more famous than you could ever imagine," Faye hissed. "Your song will be heard by millions of people." She reached over and took the sheet of music out of Mitchie's hand.

Mitchie stared down at her empty hand in shock.

At that moment, Shane walked into the cabin. "Shane!" Faye cried, racing to his side. "Babe, I've been waiting for you all morning! Man, what do you do here without a decent vente soy chai latte with extra foam?"

Mitchie snorted out loud and caught Shane's eye. Not bothering to answer Faye, he walked over to Mitchie's side. "Hey. So are you selling the song?"

"I'm not really sure," Mitchie said. "It seems like I don't have much choice." She wanted to tell him more and get his opinion, but with Faye around that seemed impossible.

Caitlyn nudged Mitchie. Holding up her wrist, she tapped her watch. She had noticed the time, and knew that Mitchie had to get to the kitchen to help out her mom.

"Look, I have to run," Mitchie said, realizing the deadline. She glanced at Faye. "This is *not* a deal yet. I'll be back after lunch, okay?"

"Sure, sure," the pop star said, keeping her

eyes on Shane. "I'll be here . . . with Shane. Right, Shane?"

"Um, sure," he said, looking confused.

"Fabulous," Faye sang out. "See you later, Mitchie."

Mitchie and Caitlyn raced out toward the kitchen. As they ran, Mitchie had to wonder, was this really about buying her song? Or was Tess right? Was Faye here to win back Shane?

Chapter Seven

When Mitchie opened the kitchen door, she could barely make her way inside. A large box, topped by smaller boxes, was blocking the entrance. "Mom?" Mitchie called out. She gently pushed a few boxes out of the way and leaned into the room, Caitlyn close behind. "Are you here?"

"Just push those over," Connie said, popping up from behind a large crate. "This is insane, isn't it?" She blew her hair out of her eyes. "If we pull this off, it will be a miracle! There are *hundreds* of people coming to this party!"

Pushing their way in, Mitchie and Caitlyn started opening boxes, unloading all the food that needed to be refrigerated. Mitchie had helped her mom do large catering events before, but she had never seen so many tiny hot dogs in her whole life!

The three of them worked hard, and soon they could see the counters and floors again. With a sigh, Connie sat down on a chair and looked over her to-do list.

"I think that's everything for now," she said, with a relieved smile. "Thanks, girls. If you hadn't helped me out, I would still be opening boxes."

Mitchie looked at her watch. She couldn't help but wonder what Faye was doing.

"Don't worry," Caitlyn said, noticing Mitchie's worried expression. She knew exactly what her friend was thinking. "We'll be back before Faye does any real harm."

"What are you talking about?" Connie asked. She put her clipboard down and leaned in closer to Mitchie. "Who is Faye?"

"Faye Hart," Mitchie said matter-of-factly.

Her mom looked at her and then at Caitlyn. "Faye 'Bubbling Sunshine' Hart?" she asked.

"Mom!" Mitchie yelped. "How do you know Faye Hart's music?"

"Everyone knows that song," her mom said, shrugging. "'*Bubbling sunshine on a summer's day,*'" she sang out.

"Oh, Mom!" Mitchie said, throwing a dish towel at her.

"I know," Connie said, "your singing talent is not from my side of the family." She reached out and pulled Mitchie into a hug.

"Your mother does make an excellent point though," Caitlyn interrupted. "Even *she* knows a Faye Hart song. Think about that Mitchie; think about your career!"

Connie put her hand up. "Hold on. What does your career have to do with Faye Hart?" She raised her eyebrows and waited for a response.

Mitchie sank down into a chair. It was time to fill in her mom. She took a deep breath. "You see, Faye came up early for Shane's party and she heard the song I wrote for B's Jam. And she liked it. And now she wants to buy it," she finished in a rush.

"She's scheduled to perform at the party," Caitlyn added. "After she heard Mitchie's song, she wanted to sing it."

"Is the song for sale, Mitchie?" Connie asked, eyeing her daughter carefully. A shiver of worry had inched its way into the back of her mind. Why would Mitchie have kept this from her?

"Honestly, I don't know," Mitchie answered. She looked up, hoping to get some good advice. Her mom usually had strong opinions that she didn't mind sharing.

For a moment, Connie didn't speak. Then she stood up. "Well, my dear," she said. "Only you can decide that. And I trust you'll come up with the right answer." She walked over to the window and grabbed a box of hamburger buns.

"That's all you are going to say?" Mitchie gasped. "No great pearls of motherly wisdom?"

"Mitchie, it's your song," her mom told her. She moved closer to her and tucked a strand of loose hair behind Mitchie's ear. "You have to decide. Just remember: you're still a kid. Any decision you make, you'll have to clear with me." She smiled and then glanced over at the large clock on the wall. "I have to keep moving. This party is starting in a few hours."

Connie had barely left when there was a knock at the back door. The door opened. Sander, Barron, Lola, and Peggy were standing on the porch.

"Hey," Barron said. "We came to get Mitchie."

"It's showtime!" Lola said, spreading her hands in front of her face dramatically.

"Well, actually it's just rehearsal," Peggy corrected her. She wasn't prepared for *showtime*—that would be a bigger deal. Peggy grabbed Mitchie's hand. "Come on. We have to be at the theater in five minutes. We're going to have the final run-through."

"Caitlyn, why don't you come with us?" Lola asked.

Mitchie was happy when Caitlyn agreed to come. While they walked, Caitlyn filled the others in on what had happened earlier with Faye. As they got closer to the theater, Mitchie felt more and more confused.

"So what are you going to do?" Lola asked when Caitlyn was finished.

Shrugging her shoulders, Mitchie sighed. She still had no answers.

Finally, they reached the theater. Opening

the door, they saw Faye in the middle of the room practicing one of her trademark dance routines. The beat of the music was familiar. It sounded similar to "Bubbling Sunshine" and other Faye Hart songs. The melody was familiar, too. Mitchie's eyes grew wide as Faye opened her mouth to sing—her lyrics!

"Wow," Barron whispered. "That didn't take long."

Mitchie walked in with her friends trailing behind her. Steve held up his hand to make sure they were all quiet as Faye continued to sing and dance in a circle, unaware that anyone had entered the theater.

"This is worse than I thought," Sander mumbled.

"Is she for real?" Barron asked as he watched Faye twirl around.

Mitchie pushed forward. "Unfortunately, I think she is," she said.

When the music ended, Faye's posse

quickly surrounded her, giving her adoring compliments. She tossed her head and took all the comments in. Finally, Faye noticed Mitchie standing off to the side.

"Hey, there," she called. "So, what do you think? We changed it a little, made the tempo a little faster." Faye winked. "And you know, added some 'Faye.' "

"That's what you call it?" Mitchie asked. Her heart was beginning to race, and her face felt hot. "That doesn't even sound like the song I wrote anymore!"

Faye walked up to Mitchie and looked her straight in the eye. "Well, no," she said calmly, "because now it's *my* song." She turned on her pointy sling backs and headed over to take a sip of bottled water.

"Now just wait a minute," Mitchie said.

Caitlyn saw the look in Mitchie's eyes and intercepted, pulling her over to the side. "Wait until you hear the offer," she whispered. "Remember? Be professional."

Mitchie took a deep breath. Caitlyn was right, she realized. But if this was what the music business was all about, she was beginning to think she didn't want any part of it.

Turning around, she faced her friends. She saw how Barron and Sander were looking at her, the concern in Caitlyn's face, and that Peggy and Lola were speechless. Suddenly, she felt a wave of sadness rush over her. It was too late.

Mitchie let her head hang down. "I can't sing it. Not at the jam, not ever." And with that she took off, running out the door before any of her friends could stop her.

Chapter Eight

Mitchie couldn't stop running. She headed toward the path that circled the lake. Her feet beat the ground in a steady motion, taking her farther and farther away from Faye. Eventually Mitchie felt her breath even out. She settled into a jog, and then sounds and scents began to filter through her sadness.

How could things have changed so

quickly? she thought. Just a day ago, she had been so happy that she had been one of the finalists for B's Jam. But now Faye had ruined everything. Her interpretation of the song had poisoned it—and made Mitchie question herself.

"Wait up!" Caitlyn shouted, interrupting Mitchie's thoughts. Mitchie stopped and turned to see Caitlyn, Barron, Sander, Lola, and Peggy jogging down the path. "We've been looking all over for you."

Mitchie lowered her head, unwilling to make eye contact.

"You *have* to sing tonight," Peggy said when they caught up to her. "The competition won't be the same without you."

"Come on," Lola added. "This jam was made for you. It's your thing. Just you and the guitar. Don't let Faye get to you."

"It's your song, Mitchie," Sander pointed out. "Why don't you sing it your way and show Faye how its done?"

Slowly, Mitchie lifted her head. She squinted across the lake, watching a group of ducks fly by. She loved this area of camp. Here, she could look out on the lake and get lost in the beauty of the place. This was where she had first thought of those lyrics for the song. She turned to face her friends.

"I'll think about it," she said softly. A smile spread across her face. "But thanks," she said. "You guys are the best."

"Well, Barron and I are," Sander said, laughing. "And we are going to win the jam, make no mistake about that."

"Oh, I don't know," Lola said, a smile tugging at the corner of her mouth. "I think that you guys have some pretty serious competition."

"You know it!" Peggy cried.

Mitchie looked down at her watch. Why was she forever running late? She had to get back to serve lunch. "I've got to go help out my mom," she said. Once more she took off, leaving her friends standing on the path, watching her run away—again.

The rest of the afternoon was a blur for Mitchie. She went to Dee's voice workshop and even got to do a little swimming. But no matter what she did to calm down, her mind was still reeling from the morning's interaction with Faye.

By late afternoon, the vibe of the camp changed once again. It seemed that everyone was rushing to take showers and get ready for the biggest party Camp Rock had ever seen. The energy in camp was on full power, and everyone was excited—everyone except Mitchie.

She avoided the whole getting-ready prep time that the rest of the camp seemed to be thriving on. Instead, she headed down to the docks, hoping that the water would relax her like it usually did.

As she walked along the wooden dock, she looked into the rowboats lined up in the water. The boats were all tied up, rocking gently with the motion of the lake. Inside the third one, Mitchie noticed a brown head of hair.

"Shane?" she asked.

Shane popped up from lying on the bottom of the boat. He lifted his sunglasses and peered up at Mitchie.

"Hey there," he said, smiling. "Fancy meeting you here."

"You hiding out, too?" she asked.

Shane sat up further. "Kinda," he confessed. He swept his hand out in a grand, regal gesture. "Would you care for a ride, m'lady?"

Mitchie giggled. "Why, yes, sir, I would love one." She climbed into the rowboat and sat facing Shane.

Rowing in a steady, rhythmic beat, Shane steered the boat out to the middle of the lake where it was quiet and still. He had gotten much better since the time on the lake when they'd gone canoeing. That time, they had ended up paddling in circles.

When they reached the middle of the lake, Shane pulled the oars inside the boat and leaned back. The sun was setting, and Shane looked so cute in the soft hues of the late-day light.

"So, what happened with Faye?" he asked, cutting to the chase.

"You brought me out to the middle of the lake to ask me that?" Mitchie teased.

"Well, if I didn't, then you would have been able to walk away from me, right?" Shane replied, smiling. "Or Faye would have figured out a way to interrupt. Now you can't escape. Smart thinking on my part, if I do say so myself."

Mitchie smiled. Sitting in the boat with Shane was the only place she wanted to be right now. She hadn't realized how much she missed talking to him. "Well, it didn't go so well," Mitchie said. Then she blurted out, "She totally changed my song!"

Shane shook his head. "Let me guess," he said, "she just added some 'Faye' to it?" He cocked his head to the side and did an impression of Faye flipping her hair.

They both laughed, and for the first time all day, Mitchie felt better.

"You know, it would be a pretty amazing opportunity for you," Shane said. He focused his brown eyes and looked directly at Mitchie. "Your song would be heard by millions of people."

"But that's the thing," Mitchie said. "It wouldn't be *my* song. It wouldn't be the song I wrote." She shrugged. "I don't know what to do."

"I think you just answered the question," Shane replied. "Now, do you have the guts to stand by your decision?"

Mitchie wished she could be as confident in herself as Shane appeared to be. "I don't know," she said, shrugging. "Maybe I'm not as talented as some people. Maybe this is the only way." Looking off into the water, she sighed, before adding, "It's just that that song means a lot to me. And so did singing it at the jam."

Shane reached over and held her hand. "Then you need to perform the song tonight," he said gently. "You are very talented, Mitchie Torres."

Mitchie looked into Shane's eyes. He made everything seem so simple!

"And," he went on, "Faye is Faye. She's one of a kind. She doesn't like to be told no, so you'll have to be strong."

"You're right," she mumbled. "I'll go talk to her."

"Of course I'm right," Shane boasted.

Mitchie reached over the side of the boat and splashed him.

"Oh, you don't want to start that!" he said. "It's a long swim back to shore."

"You wouldn't dare," Mitchie countered playfully. "One of those photographers would love to get a shot like that."

Shane ran a hand through his dark hair. "Ugh! Don't mention the shutterbugs! They are worse than the mosquitoes. I can't do anything around here without one of those long lenses zooming in on me. Believe me, I'm all for the party. But this press-conference stuff here at camp is starting to annoy me."

"You aren't prepared for them here the way you are at home," Mitchie observed.

Picking up the oars, Shane nodded. "Exactly. All summer I've been able to let my guard down. And now . . ."

Mitchie watched as the oars cut the water, pulling them back to shore. "You can't let that get in the way of celebrating going platinum," she said. "Selling all those albums is a really big deal. . . ."

"You're right," Shane said, taking in the good advice.

“Of course I’m right!” Mitchie said, repeating Shane’s earlier boast smugly.

“Now don’t get all full of yourself,” Shane warned. Winking, he guided the boat back into the open slip at the dock.

The sun had sunk below the horizon, and the bright light of day was fading. A cool purple filled the sky and made the light hazy.

“We should probably get going,” he said. “Good luck with Faye. I’m sure you’ll find the right things to say to her.”

“And good luck with everything tonight,” Mitchie told him. She stood up and jumped up on the dock. “Thanks for the ride and the pep talk.”

Shane blushed. “Sure,” he answered. He placed the oars down in the boat and stood up. “Now I gotta go play rock star.”

Just as he said that, the boat started to sway. Shane lost his balance and then . . .

SPLASH!

Mitchie laughed as she watched Shane tumble into the water. "Yeah," she said, giggling. "You're a rock star all right!"

Leaving a sputtering and soaked Shane behind, she ran up the path to her cabin. Her talk with Shane had helped. She knew what she had to do. Now she just had to find a way to tell Faye.

Chapter Nine

Mitchie walked up the path to the theater, her heart racing. Even in the privacy of her own cabin, Mitchie hadn't been able to think of what she was going to say to Faye.

When she arrived at the theater, she could hear music coming from inside the wooden walls. The beat was loud and fast. Taking a deep breath, Mitchie entered.

The scene inside was frenetic. Faye sat on

the edge of the stage, barking orders at everyone around her. Her entourage, still all dressed in black, were talking on their cell phones and running around.

There were two new people, also wearing black, who were busy with synthesizers and a drum machine. Mitchie vaguely recognized the music as her own.

Hearing the distorted chords, Mitchie suddenly knew exactly what to say. She would go with the sinple, direct approach. She walked right up to Faye. "The song is not for sale," Mitchie said, surprised at how calm her voice sounded.

Faye looked up. "I'm sorry. What did you say?" she asked. Her blue eyes held Mitchie's in a long, drawn-out stare.

Mitchie didn't back down. "I said," she recited a bit louder this time, "the song is not for sale."

Faye narrowed her eyes and glared at Mitchie. "This is crazy. Do you know how much fame you could have? Do you realize what you are doing?" She tossed her head in disgust. "You are such a novice," she said. "You have no clue."

"I think she has a pretty good clue of things to come," a voice called from the back of the theater. Turning, the girls saw Brown step out of the shadows. He came over and put a comforting arm around Mitchie. Then he looked directly at Faye. "She doesn't want to sell, so I guess that means you need to change your plans."

Faye threw her hands up in the air. "This is ridiculous. I'm so out of here."

Shane had walked in right after Brown and witnessed the entire conversation. Despite her rough exterior, Shane knew Faye could be sweet. She just cared too much about making it to the top of the industry.

"Oh, come on, Faye," he said, walking up. "Don't do this. Stay and sing tonight. Mitchie isn't trying to ruin you."

"Isn't that so sticky sweet?" Faye lashed out. "You're protecting your little songbird. Well, forget it. This place is driving me nuts. There's no decent coffee, and I've got all these mosquito bites." She looked down at her arms and pointed to several red, swollen bumps.

"There are other songs you could sing," Shane offered. Then a thought occurred to him. "This isn't about the song, is it?"

"What are you talking about?" Faye barked. "I liked the song. And you seemed to like it, too. So I thought that I'd 'Faye' it up for the party." She looked at Mitchie as if she was about to say more. Then she turned to Shane. "Listen, call me when you get back to civilization and we can hang out. I'm so over this whole back-to-nature thing." She twirled around and waved at her entourage. "Let's go, people. If we leave now, we can be at Sushi Seven for dinner." She leaned over and gave Shane two air kisses. Then she flicked a wave to Mitchie. "Have fun camper girl," she sang out.

"Well, that was something," Brown said after Faye and her entourage had cleared out of the theater. "It reminds me of a time when I was traveling with my band, the Wet Crows. . . ."

Shane put a hand on his uncle's shoulder. "Not now, Uncle Brown, huh?" He smiled and nodded toward Mitchie. "I think Mitchie probably wants to run through her song for the jam tonight."

Relieved that Faye had left and that she had her song back, Mitchie switched her focus to her performance. She was thankful for Shane and Brown's help. Now she had a jam to prepare for.

The lights had been lowered, and there were screams and hoots from the audience. B's Jam was about to start! Dee took the microphone at center stage and welcomed the campers.

"It's the annual, 'unplugged' B's Jam!" she shouted. Everyone cheered again.

"Before we begin," Dee went on, "let's have a little song for the birthday boy, shall we?"

In harmony, the entire camp sang "Happy Birthday" to Brown. He was sitting in a chair that had been decorated to look like a throne. At the end of the song, there were more cheers.

Waiting in the wings, Peggy took a deep breath. Just as she had at Final Jam last session, she was hiding out in the darkness before her performance. This time she had even more to prove. She had to show everyone she wasn't a one-hit wonder. She could nail this song, too. She spied Tess, Ella, and Lorraine sitting in the front row. She smiled. She wasn't just a backup singer anymore.

"All right," Dee said, trying to quiet the crowd. "Let's really get this jam started. As you know, there are four songs. At the end of the last song, you'll be allowed to vote for your favorite. The winner is determined by you, so listen up!"

The lights went down, and Peggy stepped out onto the stage. When she was sure her breathing was steady, she began to sing. Looking out at all the familiar faces, she felt her heart swell. They all looked so happy. This was what performing was about—making people smile. As she finished, she took a bow. Heading offstage, she went and took a seat next to Tess.

Barron and Sander stepped onto the stage right after. As always, they had a great act that showed off their music as well as their skillful dancing.

"I'm next!" Lola whispered to Mitchie. The two girls were the last ones left backstage.

"You'll be great," Mitchie said with a warm smile.

When Lola stepped onstage, Mitchie peered out into the audience. It was dark, and she could barely make out any faces.

That's probably better, she thought nervously. By the time the audience began applauding for Lola, Mitchie's hands were sweating. She grabbed her guitar.

"Hey, you're gonna be great," Shane said, appearing at her side.

"What are you doing here?" Mitchie asked. "Aren't you supposed to be at some press conference or greeting A-list stars?"

Shane laughed. "Probably! But I wouldn't have missed this jam." He looked into Mitchie's eyes. "I know this is a really big deal for you. Go out there and sell it!"

Mitchie giggled. "Never." Then she turned back to face Shane. "Thanks for being here."

"Go, go!" he urged, smiling.

Onstage there was a stool set up in front of a microphone, and Mitchie tried to get comfortable in the seat. She tilted the mike down toward her mouth.

"I'd like to dedicate this song to my friends here at camp for making me strong," she said as she started to strum the strings. She looked up, shielding her eyes from the bright lights with her hand. "Oh, and happy birthday, Brown!"

"Thank you!" Brown called out from the darkness.

The lights shifted, and Mitchie began to play. It felt surprisingly good to sing the song with the crowd clapping along. Somewhere in the middle of the second verse, she began to relax and enjoy the music. "*Yes, this is the place where I want to be,*" she sang out the last line.

A roar of applause filled the room. Mitchie got up and took a bow and then raced off the stage. She joined the other four as Dee led the audience through the voting procedure. Everyone had a ballot. They had to pick their first choice and then pass the ballots to the end of their row.

Finally, after what felt like an eternity, Dee reached up and gave Brown a folded piece of paper. The results were in. Mitchie felt Lola and Peggy grip her hands. She closed her eyes. "And the winner of B's Jam this year is . . ." Dee said, looking around the room. "Barron and Sander!"

The boys yelped and jumped up and down. They raced up onto the stage.

Mitchie couldn't help but smile. Maybe she hadn't won the jam, but she had sung her song the way she wanted. And that was victory enough.

Chapter Ten

Caitlyn couldn't believe how different Camp Rock looked. A huge white tent had been set up overlooking the lake. Twinkling lights decorated the trees, and there was a band playing. The Connect Three party was as star-studded as everyone had thought it would be.

On either side of her, Mitchie and Peggy looked as impressed as she was. Suddenly, Caitlyn laughed out loud.

"Get a look at that," she said, pointing. Tess was walking into the tent decked out in a pink slip dress with tiny sequins sewn along the edges.

"Is her camp trunk bottomless?" Mitchie asked. She was constantly impressed at the vast array of clothes Tess paraded around camp. "It's like she knew there'd be a party like this!"

"Tess is always ready for a party," Peggy agreed. "But I think that outfit is courtesy of Lorraine. The girl is a wiz with clothing. She brought two extra trunks!"

At that moment, Tess waltzed over to Mitchie. "Sorry that you didn't win the jam," she said with a sly smile. She eyed Mitchie from head to toe, taking in her jeans and sneakers. "Are you going to change before you head to the party?"

Mitchie wasn't about to let Tess ruin this night for her. Faye had come too close to doing that already. Mitchie noted that most of the guests were clad in casual jeans and T-shirts. People had really taken the camp theme to heart and had dressed the part. "Actually, Tess," she told her, "if you notice, most people are wearing jeans."

Blushing, Tess checked out the crowd. She stood up straighter and clicked her tongue. "Whatever," she said. Then she quickly walked away.

"I bet she was hoping for a walk on the red carpet in a dress like that!" Caitlyn said as she watched Tess twirl in front of Ella and Lorraine. "Too bad the only red she is going to see tonight are mosquito bites. That outfit is just calling out for those bugs."

Peggy and Mitchie laughed as they walked into the tent. Inside, there was a wooden dance floor that took up almost half of the space and a large stage with an enormous banner that read, CONGRATULATIONS CONNECT THREE. Around the sides were small white tables and chairs, and the food was set up on long banquet tables along the back. Mitchie smiled when she saw everyone enjoying the food.

"Great performance tonight, Mitchie," Colby said as she passed him.

Smiling, Mitchie thanked him. When Colby moved past her, she spotted Shane in the far corner of the tent. He was standing with Nate and Jason, greeting guests.

"Hey, let's go dance!" Lola said, dragging Caitlyn with her. "Mitchie, are you coming?" She held out her other hand to her.

Mitchie shook her head. "In a minute. There's someone I need to find." As her friends ran off, Mitchie turned around and finally saw who she was looking for. "Mom!" she cried.

"Mitchie!" her mom called out from across the tent. She came racing over. "You were amazing at the jam," Connie said as she threw her arms around Mitchie. "I am so proud of you!"

Pulling out of the hug, Mitchie studied her mom's face. "You know that I didn't win, right? Barron and Sander won."

Her mom shrugged her shoulders. "Sweetie, we both know that you won tonight. That performance was unbelievable. Mitchie, I am very proud of you." She leaned in and gave her another hug.

"Thanks," Mitchie replied. She gestured to the food presented on the tables. "Congratulations to you, too. You did it! Everyone is eating and having a good time."

Grinning, her mom nodded. "I know! Isn't it amazing? I can't believe how many stars are here!" She gasped as she took in the scene. "And they really are all enjoying my food!"

"This is a great night, Mom," Mitchie told her, nodding.

"And you know what would make it even better?" Shane asked as he came up behind her. He gave her shoulders a squeeze and whispered in her ear, "If you would sing your jam song here."

Mitchie whirled around and stared at Shane. "What?" she cried. "What are you talking about? Are you nuts?"

"I'm totally serious. Your song really captures so much about this place and this summer," Shane explained. "The guys and I would really like you to perform it here, now."

Jason and Nate appeared behind Shane. They were both smiling.

"We have an open spot with Faye leaving, so we could use your help," Nate said.

"Come on," Jason blurted out. "It will be fun!"

Mitchie turned to see her mother's face. She was nodding and smiling. Then Mitchie spun back around and looked at Shane.

"Okay!" Mitchie replied. Then her face grew serious. "On one condition."

Shane raised his right eyebrow.

"I want my friends to sing it with me," she said.

Looking to his bandmates, Shane saw Jason and Nate nod yes.

"Well, it seems we're in agreement," Shane said. "Camp Rock is up next!"

Mitchie cheered. She was so excited about telling her friends. This could be their gift to Connect Three.

A few moments later, Mitchie walked out on the stage and positioned a stool in front of the microphone. Once she was seated, she waved her arms and all the campers surrounded her.

"Congratulations to Connect Three," Mitchie said. "We'd like to dedicate this song to them and this amazing summer of music!"

Later that night, after all the celebrities had headed back to civilization, Mitchie was back in the kitchen.

"Mom, there are hardly any leftovers!" Mitchie exclaimed as she cleaned. "I'd say you scored this one right."

Smiling, her mom agreed. "It was a home run." She placed a few trays on a cart. "I'm going to take these into the freezer. You've done so much already, why don't you go hang out with your friends. I'll finish up here."

Mitchie looked at her watch. She and Shane had made a plan to meet up at the old hollowed-out tree before lights out. If she hurried, she'd be able to visit with him for a little while.

"Really?" Mitchie asked. "Are you sure?"

Connie laughed. "Yes, I'm sure. Now go!"

Mitchie ran out of the tent and across the field to the tree. She found Shane sitting on the bench, sipping a double chai latte.

"Hey. Where'd you get that?" she asked, gesturing to the drink.

Shane blushed. "A little gift from Faye. She had her driver bring it up here." He shook his head. "I'm really sorry about the whole song business. Faye can be a bit high maintenance."

"Not to mention pushy," Mitchie added.

"She's just a pop star. We can all get a little 'pushy'! But you held your ground," Shane told her. "You should be proud."

Mitchie smiled. "Thanks." She sat down next to Shane. "And thanks for asking me to sing tonight. That was really cool."

"You were great!" Shane said. He took a gulp of the chai. "I gotta tell you this stuff sure does beat the camp coffee!"

Mitchie laughed. "Can I have a sip?" He nodded and she reached over for the cup. "Do you think that I made the right decision about Faye and my song?"

"Absolutely," Shane told her. "Don't worry, one day you'll have an album that goes platinum—an album that you will have full artistic control over. I have no doubt about that."

"You think so?" Mitchie asked, feeling flattered.

"Totally," Shane said, full of confidence. "And when you do, it will be your way—and your sound."

Mitchie snuggled next to Shane and sighed. That prediction was music to her ears.

Keep rockin' with another all new story from camp!

Disney

Camp Rock

SECOND SESSION #4

Hidden Tracks

By Helen Perelman

Based on "Camp Rock," Written by Karin Gist & Regina Hicks and Julie Brown & Paul Brown

"I need chocolate!" Mitchie Torres sang out as she walked into Camp Rock's canteen. The B-Note was where campers and counselors could get treats and hang out. Located in the basement of the Mess Hall of Fame, the room was filled with old couches, tables, a vintage jukebox, and an old Ping-Pong table. There were usually a bunch of campers jamming in the corner stage area, and tonight was no exception. Just about everyone was there.

"Make that a frozen chocolate bar," Mitchie's best camp friend, Caitlyn Gellar, said, waving a hand in front of her face. Camp Rock was experiencing a heat wave—the temperatures had been over ninety-five degrees the last two days. Even though it was evening, the air was still warm and sticky. Caitlyn swept her light brown hair up off her neck into a loose ponytail.

"Definitely frozen!" Mitchie said, blowing her long, straight bangs up off her forehead. "That sounds amazing right about now."

Caitlyn smiled. Even though Mitchie was a relative Camp Rock newbie, she knew all about the perks of a frozen canteen treat. The girls had gotten incredibly close—Caitlyn was so glad that Mitchie had come to Camp Rock this summer.

As they walked over to the snack-bar window to place their orders, Caitlyn noticed Brown Cesario playing guitar. "Hey, check out Brown," she said. "He's totally jamming over there!" She pointed to the back corner of the room where their camp director was playing guitar. Their friends, Barron James and Sander Loya, two of the most talented guys at camp, were singing along with him. It was a reggae song that had a catchy melody, and Peggy Dupree and Colby Miller were singing backup. At Camp Rock you'd even find people jamming in the canteen. Caitlyn loved being at a place where there was an opportunity for creating music every moment of the day. Everyone at camp wanted to be a rock star, and this was the perfect place to learn how.

However, there was only one *official* rock star at camp. That was Shane Gray, the lead singer of the hot band, Connect Three.

Shane had met the two other members of his band at Camp Rock. They had had a pretty quick rise to fame, and Shane had gotten a bit spoiled. When he started getting bad press for his antics on a video set, his label "suggested" that he come up to camp for the summer to unwind. Brown was his uncle, so he had an easy in. This had not been Shane's idea of a good time, but the break had served him well. Not only were Connect Three's sales soaring, he was having a pretty good summer as a counselor and hanging out with the campers, especially Mitchie.

Frozen chocolate bars in hand, Mitchie and Caitlyn headed over to an old couch in the corner of the lounge. There were a few lava lamps scattered around, giving the place a warm glow. The windows were open to let in the hot summer breeze. Mitchie sighed as she settled onto the worn couch.

Even though she felt as if she were

melting, Mitchie wouldn't have wanted to be anywhere else at that moment. Thanks to her mom scoring a job as the Camp Rock cook, she'd been able to spend her whole summer there. It was a dream come true. The experience had surpassed all her expectations—especially when she met Shane.

As if on cue, Shane himself appeared at the lounge entrance. Mitchie caught his eye as he walked into the B-Note.

"Hey, there," Shane called as he crossed the room. He swung his guitar case off his shoulder and plopped down next to her on the couch, eyeing her frozen chocolate bar. "That looks pretty good," he said. "I might need one of those, too."

Before Mitchie could respond, another voiced perked up. "Do you want me to get you one?" Tess Tyler asked, rushing over to Shane. Tess was the resident camp diva. She was always surrounded by her entourage of Ella Pador and Lorraine Burgess and was constantly looking for a way to get close to Shane.

"Lorraine," she barked to the redheaded girl behind her. "Go get Shane one of those."

Lorraine was a relatively new member of Tess's entourage. She'd arrived for Second Session and, when she moved into Vibe Cabin, had quickly fallen in as one of Tess's adoring fans.

When Mitchie first came to Camp Rock, she wanted to be part of that group, too. Mitchie had even told a huge lie about her mother being a famous music executive so that Tess would be impressed. But Mitchie had quickly learned that lying was not the best way to make friends at camp. When everyone found out the truth, Mitchie got to see who her real friends at camp were—and Tess was not one of them!

But Caitlyn was. Now, she and Mitchie exchanged smirks at Tess's latest attempt to cozy up to Shane.

"I'll get it. Thanks anyway," Shane told Tess, standing up. He went up to the snack-bar window. A few minutes later, he returned with his own frozen treat and sat down next to Mitchie once again.

"How was your meeting with Dee?" Mitchie asked. She had seen Shane and a few other full-time counselors sitting with Dee La Duke, Camp Rock's musical director, after dinner. It looked as if they were plotting something big.

"Long," Shane sighed. "And we still didn't finish! I never knew how much planning goes into each Camp Rock activity. And I'm just a guest instructor!"

"Well we thank you for all your hard work!" Caitlyn said, grinning.

Shane smiled and looked over at Brown. "So listen, after my uncle finishes, I'd like to play a new tune for you guys," he said.

"Great!' Mitchie said. She loved listening to Shane sing. And if he had a new song, she definitely wanted to hear it.

Shane's thick, dark eyebrows arched. "I think you'll like it, but you'll have to be totally honest with me."

"You got it," Mitchie and Caitlyn agreed, nodding.

"This new album has to be really good," Shane went on. "There's a lot of pressure now."

Connect Three's latest album had recently gone platinum. It was a huge deal and everyone was thrilled, but Mitchie knew Shane was concerned about the band's follow-up effort. It had to be great.

Shane leaned down to open his guitar case. "Our producer is all over us about making this CD special."

Just then, Lola Scott walked over and sat on the floor. She looked up at Shane as he tuned his guitar. "Hey, Shane, are you going to play next?" Lola was a veteran at Camp Rock. She had been singing since she was a little girl. Her mother was a big-time Broadway star, and Lola had inherited her talent and flare.

Shane nodded. "Yeah, we're back in the studio at the end of the summer, and I have to finish some songs," he said. "I was hoping that you guys would be my first audience."

Trying to hide her excitement, Lola nodded her head yes. Who wouldn't want to be the first to hear a Shane Gray original?

"Is it about camp?" Caitlyn asked. She leaned forward in her seat, wanting to get the full scoop.

"Kinda," Shane replied mysteriously. "You could say that I have been heavily influenced here." He looked over at Mitchie and smiled.

"Ooooh!" Lola cried, seeing how Shane looked at Michie. "Is it a love song?"

Mitchie pushed Lola with her feet. "Lola!" she scolded, feeling her face turn a bright beet red.

Shane just laughed. "No! No! It's simpler than that. It's about the summer nights here at camp."

"You mean the superhot summer nights and how we're all going to dehydrate?" Caitlyn asked. She began using her hand as a fan. "This heat is killing me!"

Lola nodded and took a sip of her ice water. "It's supposed to break tomorrow," she said. "But first we have to make it through tonight!"

"I still can't believe there is no air-conditioning here," Tess said, joining the conversation. Lorraine and Ella were right behind her holding matching ice-cream cones. All of them had one of their hands on their hips, their glossy lips pouting. "This is just not humane. I'm melting!"

"Didn't the Wicked Witch of the West say that?" Caitlyn asked Mitchie, smiling.

Mitchie stifled a giggle with her hand as Tess spun and turned away. "Good one,

Caitlyn," she threw back over her shoulder.

"Aw, come on," Lola said, laughing. "It isn't so bad. It's camp, people!"

"Lola's right," Shane chimed in. "Plus, where else would you hear crickets like this?" He gestured toward the three open windows behind the couches. "Isn't that a cool sound?"

Mitchie smiled. The old Shane would never have noticed that! She was glad that he was feeling more relaxed now that it was Second Session. He might have missed the glamorous A-list life, but he definitely knew how to enjoy the peaceful lakeside camp.

"It's great background for a song, don't you think?" Shane said as he tapped his guitar to the cricket beat.

Just then, Brown and the others stopped playing, and the cricket chorus grew even louder.

"You should lay that down as a track on your new CD," Mitchie joked. "Then it would have something special—a Camp Rock special tribute."

Standing up, Shane walked over to the window. He turned and looked around the room. A smile spread across his face. "That's an amazing idea," he said. "Mitchie, you're brilliant!"

"What's brilliant?" Peggy asked, joining the group. Now that her set with Brown and the boys was over she was ready to have a frozen treat with her friends. "The song that we just sang?" She winked at Barron and Sander and did a little curtsy. Ever since Peggy had won Final Jam and stopped being Tess's backup singer, she had been enjoying singing on her own. While she loved being a solo vocalist, jamming with Brown, Sander, and Colby was fun, too.

"You sounded great," Lola told Peggy. "But I don't think Shane was talking about that song. He seems to have some other idea in his head."

Shane ran back over to the couch and packed up his guitar. After he snapped the case shut, he turned to Mitchie.

"Seriously, Mitchie," he said. "Thank you for saving me!" Turning, he dashed out the door.

"What was that all about?" Peggy asked, totally bewildered. "What did I miss?"

"I have no idea," Mitchie confessed. What had she said to inspire Shane? And when would they hear his new song?